Bop! Pow! Bang! Smack! Zo
stamping. But when he upsets ɑ
boot's on the other foot!

Jenny Nimmo worked at the BBC for a number of years, ending in a spell as a director/adaptor for "Jackanory". Her many books for children include *The Owl-Tree* (Winner of the Smarties Book Prize Gold Award), *The Stone Mouse* (shortlisted for the Carnegie Medal and broadcast on BBC TV) and a trilogy, *The Snow Spider* (Winner of the Smarties Book Prize), *Emlyn's Moon* and *The Chestnut Soldier* – all three of which have been made into television series. Jenny Nimmo lives in a converted watermill in Wales with her artist husband and three children.

David Parkins has illustrated several children's books, including six Sophie stories, *No Problem*, *Tick-Tock*, *Prowlpuss* (shortlisted for the Kurt Maschler Award and the Smarties Book Prize) and *Aunt Nancy and Old Man Trouble*. He also illustrates the *Beano's* Billy-Whizz comic-strip.

Books by the same author

The Chestnut Soldier

Emlyn's Moon

The Snow Spider

The Stone Mouse

JENNY NIMMO

RONNIE and the GIANT MILLIPEDE

Illustrations by David Parkins

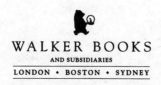

WALKER BOOKS

AND SUBSIDIARIES

LONDON • BOSTON • SYDNEY

First published 1995 by
Walker Books Ltd, 87 Vauxhall Walk
London SE11 5HJ

This edition published 1996

4 6 8 10 9 7 5 3

Text © 1995 Jenny Nimmo
Illustrations © 1995 David Parkins

This book has been typeset in Garamond.

Printed in England

British Library Cataloguing in Publication Data
A catalogue record for this book
is available from the British Library.

ISBN 0-7445-4740-7

CONTENTS

THE STAMPING BEGINS

HAPPY BIRTHDAY RONNIE x

Ronnie Stiltskin was given a new pair of boots for his seventh birthday. They were black with thick, heavy soles and Ronnie was very proud of them. He thought he'd try them out on a peanut someone had dropped on the kitchen floor, and brought his foot down **CRASH!** on to the tiles.

The noise was music to Ronnie's ears and he decided that stamping was the greatest thing in the world.

Next day Ronnie stamped on an empty orange-juice carton which gave a very pleasing *POP!* and made several girls scream.

POP!

Then he spied an
empty Coke can.
It made a terrific
BANG! when
Ronnie stamped
on it, and nearly
made a boy fall
off his bike.

A half-full packet
of crisps outside
Ronnie's gate
wasn't quite so
satisfactory, but
the smashed
crisps crackled
enough to frighten
Ronnie's cat, Charlie.

There was nothing on the kitchen
floor for Ronnie to stamp on so he
blew up a paper bag, tied the top
with a rubber band and jumped on it.
It made the best **BoP!** ever.

Mrs Stiltskin was so frightened
she dropped a pan of chips,
and Mr Stiltskin accidentally tore
his newspaper in half.

Charlie the cat thought seriously about moving in with the people next door, a nice old couple who never made a noise.

"Ronnie!" roared Mr Stiltskin. "This stamping has got to stop!"

But after tea he saw that his mother had dropped a grape right in front of the kitchen sink, so he stamped on that. *Smush! Squish!* Seeds and green flesh shot across the floor and stuck to the wall.

"Ronnie!" screamed Mrs Stiltskin. "Stop stamping! You know what happened to Rumpel!"

Rumpel Stiltskin, your ancestor.
He stamped so hard he went right through
the floor.

That must have been
in the olden days,
when floors weren't
very strong.

After this Ronnie tried not to
stamp for a whole day.

15

But then he went to his friend
Bob's birthday party, and there
were all these balloons lying about,
just asking to be stamped on.

Bob's granny thought another war had started and her legs gave way completely.  But Ronnie was having such a good time bursting balloons, he didn't hear Bob's mother shouting at him. He didn't even see Bob's granny being carried upstairs.

When Mrs Stiltskin came to collect Ronnie, Bob's mother said, "We don't want Ronnie round here any more."

CHARLIE LEAVES HOME

Mrs Stiltskin thought that Ronnie
had learned his lesson. But he hadn't.
On the way home from Bob's
house, he stamped on an ice-cream
someone had dropped. It stuck to
his boots and he walked it all over
the hall carpet.

Mrs Stiltskin took Ronnie's boots away and made him wear his slippers. But he stamped on a nail that went right through to his foot.

The doctor said Ronnie ought to wear boots if he was the sort of boy who stamped on things.

Mrs Stiltskin tried to explain how noisy boots were, but the doctor said, "It's better than having holes in your feet."

Mr and Mrs Stiltskin became very depressed. They made Ronnie stay in the garden as much as possible. At least the noise wasn't so close.

Ronnie stamped on stones…

 he stamped on molehills…

and bonfires, on dustbin lids…

and broken flower pots, and clothes pegs.

He even stamped on the crazy paving, and made it really crazy.

Charlie the cat spent the
day at the top of a very
tall tree.
When Mr and Mrs Stiltskin let
Ronnie in for the night, they
made him take
off his boots and
leave them
outside.

But before he
went to bed,
Ronnie stamped
on his pillow
to make it comfy;

he stamped on the
toothpaste tube
to make the tooth-
paste ooze out;

and he stamped
on his clothes
so that they should
be nicely pressed
for the morning.

Mr and Mrs Stiltskin went quite hoarse from shouting at Ronnie. Their throats were so sore, they couldn't speak for a whole day, and had to write notes to each other.

Charlie the cat went to live with the people next door.

A DANGEROUS PLACE

The people who lived in Ronnie's street became very unfriendly, so the Stiltskins decided to move away. They bought an old cottage, outside town, where there were no neighbours to complain about the noise.

Mr Stiltskin had to build a new kitchen. The old one was too small and the floorboards were rotten. He bricked up the doors and warned Ronnie to keep away.

But Ronnie couldn't resist taking
a peek. The windows had fallen
out and wet leaves had floated in,
making the room wet and musty.
Hundreds of tiny creatures had
made their homes in damp, dark
corners.

Ronnie climbed through the broken window and tried out the floorboards.

What a delicious noise! Ronnie sang with joy.

Soon a trail of wounded and unhappy creatures began to leave the old kitchen. Their homes were gone (not to mention their children). Ronnie didn't even notice them. He was having such fun.

And then a voice said:

Ronnie, caught in mid-stamp,
saw a little man looking through the
broken window. He wore a red
nightcap and his long nose rested
on the sill. His skin was as wrinkled
as a prune.

"All this stamping has got to stop," said the little man. "I know it's fun, but it never does you any good. I learned the hard way."

Who's going to stop me?

The millipede.

"Millipedes aren't dangerous," scoffed Ronnie. "They're teeny weeny things."

"They grow," the stranger told him. "They grow to be ENORMOUS. And they've got hundreds and hundreds of feet. I wouldn't like you to come to grief!"

And with that he vanished.

Ronnie peered into the shadowy corners of the old kitchen. He began to imagine giant THINGS lurking there, and ran out, fast.

31

"I just saw a tiny man with a wrinkled face," panted Ronnie, "and he was wearing a red hat like a sock. He told me there was a giant millipede living here."

"Sounds like Rumpel Stiltskin," said Ronnie's father. "But he died four hundred years ago. And as for giant millipedes, they live only in jungles."

Ronnie wasn't so sure. He decided that if millipedes grew to be enormous, he'd better stop them growing before they got too big to handle.

RONNIE MAKES A PROMISE

Later that day, Ronnie saw a
millipede slipping between the milk
bottles on the step. He swung his
foot out – but too late to get the
millipede. Too late to avoid the
bottles. Crack! Tinkle! They flew
into the air and smashed on to the
path.

While he was sweeping up the
broken glass, Ronnie saw the
millipede creeping under a ladder.
Ronnie dropped his broom and
leapt for the millipede.

He missed the millipede but he didn't miss the ladder. *CLONK!* *SMASH!* It slipped down the wall and went straight through the sitting-room window.

"We were going to take you to the seaside this weekend," said Mr Stiltskin. "But not if you do any more stamping."

The beach was one of Ronnie's favourite places. There were so many things to stamp on. Limpets to CRUNCH! shells to CRACK! old cans to BANG! and pools to SPLOSH! in. How could Ronnie bear to miss it?

"I promise not to stamp on anything again," said Ronnie breathlessly.

He closed his eyes, wondering how he could keep his promise.

RONNIE MEETS RUMPEL

Ronnie didn't stamp on anything
for the rest of that day. But it was
agony. His feet ached with not
stamping. They itched and burned
and throbbed with not treading
hard on anything.

At teatime Ronnie had to twist his feet round the legs of his chair so they wouldn't be tempted by so much as a crumb.

Have you got toothache, Ronnie?

No, but my feet are killing me.

When he went to bed he dreamed that he had the biggest feet in the world, and they THUMPED! and BOOMED! even when he walked on tiptoe.

"Wake up!" said a cross voice.

Ronnie opened his eyes. There, sitting on the end of his bed, was the little man in the red nightcap. "Are ... are you Rumpel Stiltskin?" Ronnie asked.

"Right first time," said the little man. "I came to warn you, Ronnie. Don't you remember my story?"

Not exactly.

Well, I'll tell you.

"There was a girl, and she asked me to spin flax into gold for her, so that the King would marry her. I agreed and she promised to give me her first child as a reward."

"That wretched girl broke her word. The King married her but she refused to hand over their baby. So I gave her another chance; I said if she guessed my name in three days she could keep the child."

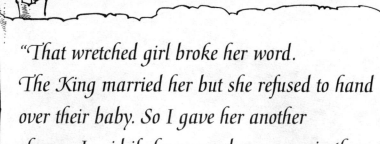

"Well, she guessed right. I was that mad I stamped so hard I went right through the floor. Down, down, down I fell into a deep, dark pit!"

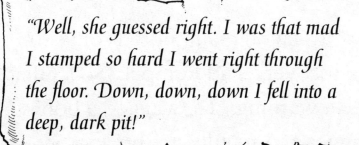

"It's taken me hundreds of years to recover," said Rumpel. "So let that be a warning." He wagged a bony finger and scuttled to the door.

"Hold on," said Ronnie.

What about the millipede?

"What was all that about a giant millipede?"

Rumpel gave Ronnie a funny wink, and then he vanished.

Ronnie lay in bed thinking about what his ancestor had told him. He tried to keep his feet still, but they had a mind of their own.

CLANK! CLONK! CLANK! CLONK!

went the bedsprings.

His father banged on the wall.

Ronnie, be quiet or you won't go to the beach!

Please!

And then Ronnie had a brilliant idea. He would go to the old kitchen. It was right on the other side of the house and he could make as much noise as he wanted. His parents would never hear him. As for giant millipedes – they lived only in jungles – didn't they? Why should he believe a tiny man who was hundreds of years old?

A MIDNIGHT RUMPUS

Ronnie tiptoed past his parents'
bedroom, carrying his boots. He
didn't even have to switch the light
on, because it was such a bright
moonlit night.

In the kitchen he lifted
the bag out of the
waste-bin; it was full
of lovely things to
stamp on. Ronnie put it
over his shoulder and
crept out of the house.
When he reached the window
of the *old* kitchen, he poured
his rubbish across
the floor. Cartons,
cans, boxes, bottles,
polythene packaging
and empty kitchen
towel tubes were
spread before him
like a feast.

Ronnie pulled on his boots.
"Yippee!" he yelled and leapt
through the window.

Ronnie bounced, stamped, crashed,
cracked and shrieked with glee.

A deafening rumpus poured from
the old kitchen, but no one heard it.

Creatures buzzed, screamed, whizzed and fluttered in all directions, but no one heard them. And no one heard Ronnie's howl of delight or the dreadful thudding of his murderous black boots.

All too soon everything had been smashed so flat that no sound could be heard except for a pathetic SQUISH! SQUASH! SQUIDDLE! And a long sigh from the tired old floorboards.

And then Ronnie saw the millipede. It was right in the middle of the floor, bathed in moonlight.

Ronnie couldn't help himself. With a mighty spring he leapt towards the tiny creature. But the millipede rolled to safety and Ronnie crashed onto empty floorboards.

The old boards split. And down
went Ronnie, into a deep, dark pit!

THE MILLIPEDE'S REVENGE

As Ronnie lay there, staring up at the hole he'd tumbled through, something moved into the path of moonlight. Something HUGE!

Clinging to a thick cobweb the
thing began to swing down towards
Ronnie. Closer and closer. And
now Ronnie could see that it had
hundreds of feet. Hundreds and
hundreds and hundreds.

It was a giant millipede!

"Oooooo! P-p-please don't stamp on me. I didn't mean to hurt your baby. Honestly I didn't!"

But the millipede kept coming.

No one heard him. And with one last dreadful wail, the terrified Ronnie fainted clean away.

Next morning Mr and Mrs Stiltskin searched for Ronnie everywhere. They called and called, but Ronnie couldn't answer – he'd lost his voice. In the end they rang the police. And then Mr Stiltskin remembered the old kitchen.

When they pulled Ronnie out of the cellar he was covered in bruises – six hundred and fifty, to be precise.

A millipede stamped on me.

Mr Stiltskin was not sympathetic. "You fell into a cellar full of junk, that's what you did," he said. "I told you that place was dangerous, didn't I?"

"Yes, Dad," whispered Ronnie.

The newspapers heard of Ronnie's ordeal and printed his story.

FRE
New
witr
fro
a

sp
bu
th
if
we
fro

RONNIE STILTSKIN IS FOUND ALIVE AFTER FALLING INTO THE CELLAR.

HE CLAIMS he was stamped on by a giant millipede. When we asked Ronnie what he had learned from his experience, he said, "It hurt a lot. Stamping on things is wicked. I would never do a thing like that!"

Ronnie never stamped on
anything again. And he never saw
Rumpel Stiltskin.

Except once!

MORE WALKER SPRINTERS
For You to Enjoy

☐ 0-7445-4739-3   *Posh Watson*
by Gillian Cross/Mike Gordon   £3.50

☐ 0-7445-4300-2   *Little Stupendo*
by Jon Blake/
Martin Chatterton   £3.50

☐ 0-7445-4375-4   *Oliver Sundew, Tooth Fairy*
by Sam McBratney/
Dom Mansell   £3.50

☐ 0-7445-3686-3   *The Magic Boathouse*
by Sam Llewellyn/
Arthur Robins   £3.50

☐ 0-7445-3699-5   *Fighting Dragons*
by Colin West   £3.50

☐ 0-7445-3687-1   *Hector the Rat*
by Tony Wilkinson   £3.50

☐ 0-7445-3091-1   *The Finger-eater*
by Dick King-Smith/
Arthur Robins   £3.50

Name ──────────────────────────────────

Address ────────────────────────────────

──